Anime Pets

Escritia Online

Escritia.com

ISBN: **9798861442343**

2022 Manchester, United Kingdom

Escritia.com

Visit our website and find our products and news.

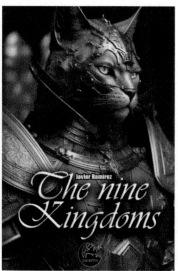

Escritia.com

Visit our website and find our products and news.

Printed in Great Britain
by Amazon